CLEAN AIR

BY ELIZABETH THOMAS

Published by The Child's World®
1980 Lookout Drive • Mankato, MN 56003-1705
800-599-READ • www.childsworld.com

PHOTO CREDITS
Bartosz Hadyniak/iStockphoto, cover, 1; S. Greg Panosian/
iStockphoto, 5; Shutterstock Images, 7, 25, 29; Fernando Carniel
Machado/iStockphoto, 9; Geoffrey Kuchera/Shutterstock Images, 11;
Eleonora Kolomiyets/Shutterstock Images, 13; Joe Gough/Shutterstock
Images, 15; Alexander Raths/iStockphoto, 17; iStockphoto, 19, 27;
Olga Anourina/iStockphoto, 21; Chanyut Sribua-rawd/iStockphoto, 23

CONTENT CONSULTANT
Jacques Finlay, Associate Professor, Department of Ecology,
Evolution and Behavior, University of Minnesota

ACKNOWLEDGMENTS
The Child's World®: Mary Berendes, Publishing Director
The Design Lab: Design
Red Line Editorial: Editorial direction

ISBN: 978-1-60973-170-0
LCCN: 2011927666

Printed in the United States of America in Mankato, MN
July, 2011
PA02090

TABLE OF CONTENTS

THE AIR WE BREATHE

Air pollution is a major concern for our environment. Many people are working to decrease two main kinds of air pollution. One kind includes gases and dust that make the air dirty. The other kind includes **greenhouse gases**, with carbon dioxide as the leader. These gases trap heat inside the **atmosphere** the way windows trap heat inside a car in a sunny parking lot. This causes **global warming**.

Most air pollution comes from burning **fossil fuels**. These are oil, natural gas, and coal.

Gasoline comes from oil. Gas-powered vehicles are the number one source of air

There are many easy ways to help keep Earth's air clear and clean.

pollution. Power plants that burn coal to make electricity are another huge source. Chemical plants, steel mills, and plastic factories are also causes.

But there is so much you can do to help reduce air pollution. Helping Earth can be easy and fun!

TIP #1

SKIP THE CAR

An easy way to help keep air clean is to walk or ride your bike somewhere. If you're going to soccer practice a few blocks away from your home, ride your bike instead of getting a ride from your parents. You and your family could also take a bus instead of using the car.

WHY?

Forty percent of all car trips travel less than 2 miles (3.2 km). Imagine if everyone in the United States took one less car trip a week. We would save 149 million tons (135 million t) of gas **emissions** from going into the atmosphere.

Riding bikes instead of driving cars is good exercise, saves gas, and helps keep the air clean.

7

RECYCLE!

Did you know that more than one third of all garbage can be recycled? Recycle glass, aluminum, cardboard, paper, and plastic. Keeping these items out of garbage burners means less **pollutants** will go into the air. It also means that fewer raw materials need to be taken from Earth to make more of these items.

WHY?

Paper comes from trees. Trees help keep air clean. They breathe in carbon dioxide and release oxygen back into the air. The more we recycle paper, the fewer trees we need to cut down.

Aluminum from old cans can be made into new cans.

TIP #3

TURN IT OFF

When you leave a room, make sure the lights are off. Remember to turn off the computer and television when you're done using them. Turn off other electronics when you are finished using them, too.

WHY?

This will help save electricity. In many cases, it is made by burning coal or natural gas. The less electricity we use, the less natural gas will be burned. And the cleaner our air will be!

By turning off the lights when you leave a room, you can also help your family save money on electricity bills.

TURN GREASE INTO FUEL

In 2009, a group of middle school students in Rhode Island decided to help stop global warming. They formed Project T.G.I.F., or Turn Grease into Fuel. They collected cooking oil from restaurants that was going to be thrown away. Then, they brought it to a biodiesel refinery, where it was turned into biofuel. In 2009, the oil they collected made 30,000 gallons (114,000 L) of biofuel. About 600,000 pounds (272,000 kg) of carbon dioxide were not added to the atmosphere because of their work!

CLEAN SCHOOL BUSES

More than 24 million kids ride school buses every day in the United States. That means a lot of gasoline emissions. Find out from your teacher or principal how old your school's buses are. If they were built before 1990, they pollute the air more than they should. The US Environmental Protection Agency has a program called Clean School Bus USA. Check it out to see how you can help your school's buses pollute less.

WHY?

School buses travel about 4 billion miles (6 billion km) each year taking kids to and from school. If the buses use diesel fuel, they can give off about 3,000 tons (2,722 t) of soot. About 95,000 tons (86,183 t) of other pollutants go into the atmosphere, too.

School buses travel many miles each day bringing students to and from school.

PLANT YOUR OWN FRUITS AND VEGGIES

Collect seeds from tomatoes, beans, and raspberries. Fill small pots with soil. Plant each pot with different seeds. Push the seeds in the soil about half an inch (1.2 cm). Put each pot in a plastic bag and tie it shut. Place the pots in a warm place. Wait for the seeds to sprout. When it is warm enough outside, put your plants in a garden.

WHY?

Fruits and vegetables have to be shipped to your local store. Sometimes they travel from far away. The airplanes, ships, trains, and trucks that bring these foods to you burn fossil fuels. Growing your favorite foods means you'll contribute less to these pollutants going into the air.

Growing your own vegetables can be tasty, fun, and good for the environment!

PLANT A TREE

Dig a hole as deep as the new tree's root ball and twice as wide. Spread out the roots. If the tree's roots are tied up, cut the rope. Place the root ball in the hole. Fill in the hole with soil and pack it down. Water the tree until the soil is soaked. Pile mulch around the trunk of the tree. Water the tree often.

WHY?

It is harmful for people to breathe too much carbon dioxide. But trees need it to live. Trees also make oxygen. So, they add fresh air to the atmosphere. They also provide shade. If you plant one near your house, you might not need to use the air conditioning as much. This means less fossil fuel will be burned.

Cutting any ropes around a tree's root ball will allow the roots to spread out.

PLANTING AND RAISING AWARENESS

When the fourth graders of Cornell Grade School learned that some of the trees and plants native to Illinois were in danger of dying out, they decided to do something about it. They planted six kinds of plants that were threatened. They also planned an outdoor preservation area, where the plants would not be disturbed. For all their hard work, the class won the 2010 Illinois Environmental Protection Agency's Green Youth Award.

TIP #7

MAKE YOUR OWN CLEANING PRODUCTS

Help prevent indoor air pollution by mixing up a batch of your own cleaners using safe, natural products. It's easy to make glass cleaner. Just pour vinegar into a spray bottle until it is half full. Fill the rest of the bottle with water. Shake to mix. Use it to clean mirrors, windows, and glass tabletops.

WHY?

Air pollution doesn't just happen outside. Indoor air quality is often two to five times worse than the air outdoors. One reason for this is because some household cleaning supplies contain chemicals that go into the air. Natural products like vinegar, soap, baking soda, or lemon juice can help keep your house and air clean.

You can make your own cleaning solution with things you have around the house, such as vinegar or lemon juice.

USE YOUR OWN POWER!

Help keep air clean while you do chores around your home. Use a push mower to cut the grass instead of a gas or electric mower. Use a rake instead of a leaf blower to rake the leaves that fall on the yard. Build your muscles. Use a shovel to clear snow off the steps and sidewalk instead of using a snowblower.

WHY?

Using your own power will save gasoline. Then fewer gasoline emissions get into the air. By using your own energy, you are helping keep the air clean.

Raking leaves in the fall is fun. You can jump in them when you're done, too!

DRY THE NATURAL WAY

Hang your clothes outside on a clothesline instead of tossing them in the dryer. Your clothes will dry from the sun's warmth and the blowing breeze. And they'll smell like the outdoors, too! You can string a clothesline indoors if it is raining.

WHY?

Clothes dryers use nearly 1 million watt-hours (1,000 kWh) of electricity each year. Most electricity in the United States is made by burning fossil fuels. Drying your clothes naturally will keep more pollutants out of the air.

Drying your clothes naturally can help them stay in good shape so they last a long time.

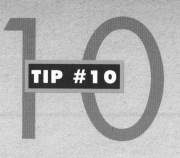

TIP #10

COMPOST IT!

Making **compost** keeps garbage out of landfills. Here's how to make your own:

Pick a place in the yard. Start the pile with food scraps. Don't use any meat or dairy. Then mix in grass clippings and leaves. This layer should be about a foot (.3 m) deep. Add about an inch (2.5 cm) of garden soil and an inch or two (2.5–5 cm) of soil from the yard. Turn the compost every week with a shovel. In three or four months, you'll have great natural fertilizer for your garden.

WHY?

You are keeping waste that can be used as compost from being buried in landfills. Putting this waste in landfills leads to methane gas production. Too much methane in the atmosphere contributes to global warming.

Using compost as fertilizer can help put nutrients back into the soil. These nutrients help plants grow well.

COOL IT WITH THE VIDEO GAMES!

Playing video or computer games is a lot of fun, but too many hours spent doing these activities uses a lot of energy. Feel how hot the computer or television is after a few hours of playing? Cut back on the virtual games and play a game outside.

WHY?

Playing video or computer games uses more energy than watching television or working on the computer. That means even more fossil fuel has to be burned to create electricity.

For every minute you spend playing a video game, try spending the same amount of time playing outside.

NO IDLING

Organize a "no **idling**" campaign at your school. Parents should turn off their cars when they have to wait more than 30 seconds to pick up their kids. Put signs up in the parking lot and by the drop-off area. Let parents know that ten seconds of idling can use more fuel than turning the engine off and restarting it. They'll want to turn their cars off!

WHY?

A car idling for just ten minutes burns up less than one-tenth of a gallon (.38 L) of gas. That might not seem like a lot, but it adds up! Over weeks and months, fumes from an idling car add a lot of pollutants into the air.

Automobiles produce pollutants that can harm air quality.

MORE WAYS TO GO GREEN

1. **Join** the Environmental Kids Club for games and activities, projects, news, and more from the Environmental Protection Agency.

2. **Put** a plant in a room at school or at home. This will help keep the indoor air clean.

3. **Make** sure that your family and school get rid of hazardous waste correctly. Hazardous waste includes batteries, paint, electronics, and old medicine.

4. **When** dusting or cleaning your room, use rags instead of paper towels or disposable cloths.

5. **Wear** a sweater! In cool weather, keep the heat turned down during the day and down even lower at night.

6. **In** the summer, turn on the fans instead of the air conditioning.

7. **Plant** a wildflower garden. The plants will clean the air and the flowers will make it smell sweet!

8. **Ask** your parents to take clothes to a dry cleaner that does not use toxic chemicals for cleaning.

9. **Let** your elected officials in the city, state, and federal government know that you support action for clean air.

10. **Write** a letter to your local newspaper describing what you and your friends are doing to help reduce air pollution.

11. **Volunteer** to help clean a park or join a group that is planting trees or gardens in your city.

12. **Share** these tips for keeping the air clean with your friends, family, and classmates. Ask them to join you in going green!

atmosphere (AT-muss-feer): The atmosphere is the layer of gases around Earth. Air pollution affects the atmosphere.

biofuel (BY-oh-fyoo-ul): Biofuel is fuel that is made from raw biological materials. Biofuel pollutes the air less than fossil fuel.

compost (KOM-pohst): Compost is a mixture of leaves, old food scraps, and soil that is used to fertilize plants and land. You can make compost to reduce waste that goes to landfills.

emissions (i-MISH-uns): Emissions are the release of things, such as chemicals into the atmosphere. Gasoline emissions from cars pollute the atmosphere.

fossil fuels (FOSS-ul FYOO-uls): Fossil fuels are oil, natural gas, and coal, which formed from the remains of ancient plants. Burning fossil fuels causes air pollution.

global warming (GLOHB-ul WOR-ming): Global warming is the heating up of Earth's atmosphere and oceans due to air pollution. Too much carbon dioxide in the air contributes to global warming.

greenhouse gases (GREEN-houss GASS-es): Greenhouse gases are gases like carbon dioxide and methane that help hold heat in the atmosphere. Too many greenhouse gases in the atmosphere contribute to global warming.

idling (EYE-dul-ing): Something that is idling is running slowly. An idling car contributes to air pollution.

pollutants (puh-LOOT-unts): Pollutants are things that pollute. Burning garbage sends pollutants into the air.

FURTHER READING

BOOKS

Burne, David. *Earth Watch*. New York: DK, 2001.

Jankeliowitch, Anne. *50 Ways to Save the Earth*. New York: Abram Books, 2008.

Suzuki, David. *Eco-Fun: Great Projects, Experiments, and Games for a Greener Earth*. Vancouver: Greystone Books, 2001.

WEB SITES

Visit our Web site for links about clean air:
http://www.childsworld.com/links

Note to Parents, Teachers, and Librarians: We routinely verify our Web links to make sure they are safe and active sites. So encourage your readers to check them out!

INDEX